SANTA'S DIRTY BIKERS

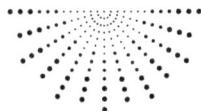

SARWAH CREED

Copyright © 2022 by Sarwah Creed

All rights reserved.

No part of this book may be reproduced in any form or by any electronic or mechanical means, including information storage and retrieval systems, without written permission from the author, except for the use of brief quotations in a book review.

❀ Created with Vellum

Copyright © 2022 by Sarwah Creed

All rights reserved.

No part of this book may be reproduced in any form or by any electronic or mechanical means, including information storage and retrieval systems, without written permission from the author, except for the use of brief quotations in a book review.

❦ Created with Vellum

ABOUT SARWAH CREED

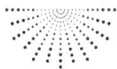

Sarwah Creed is the author of The FlirtChat series. When she's not writing, she's running, reading, or listening to music. She lives with her three children in Madrid.

Learn more about Sarwah by connecting with her on social media:

Newsletter ---- http://eepurl.com/g0cLoH

ABOUT THE F*** UNDER THE MISTLETOE SERIES

F* Under the Mistletoe is a 6 book collection series by Poppy Flynn, Sarwah Creed, Sylvie Haas, Kylie Love & Alys Fraser.**

A collection of standalone novels from New Adult, Stepbrother, OMYW, Mafia, and Second Chance Romance. There is something for every reader in this amazing reverse harem series!

One-Night Stand by Sarwah Creed
I went to Vegas and hit the roulette table. I lost a bet, not to one guy but all three.

Sparkles and Spankings by Sylvie Haas

Going for top dollar at the charity auction feels like a win, but the three highest bidders have an even better proposition for me.

Basic Instinct by Poppy Flynn

A staff Christmas party in a kink dungeon is one thing... getting caught under the mistletoe by three of her colleagues? Well that was an entirely different matter!

Three Santas & I

One curvy girl, three hung Santas... Christmas will be torrid this year!

Holly's Mistletoe Mafia

When she finds herself in the wrong place at the wrong time, three Mr. Rights make Holly an offer she can't refuse.

Santa's Dirty Bikers by Sarwah Creed

Tired of being good, Amber decides to get down and dirty with Santa's bikers.

ABOUT SANTA'S DIRTY BIKERS

Tired of being the good girl, Amber decides to get down and dirty with Santa's bikers.

Happy Christmas to me: my boyfriend was cheating on me. No festive proposal this year, then.

I was miles from home, with no flights available, on Christmas Eve.

Damn.

A sexy biker, Beau, offered me a ride to his house and I jumped on—tired of always doing the right thing. I'd done that, up until now, only to have my heart broken into so many pieces. Beau introduced me to his brothers, Adrian and Austin.

The brothers wanted to do more than just a kiss under the mistletoe. I was happy to assist in so many filthy ways. It was as if our fun had ended as quickly as it had begun.

I wanted more, but I was scared of admitting it and having my heart broken again...

Author's Note:
This is a kinky stand-alone novella about a

single girl who gets more than she bargained for on Christmas day.

There is an HEA.

1
AMBER

"Mom, I know. I'm going to surprise Dominic in Alaska."

I could hear her repeating exactly what I'd said to her a few minutes ago. I was packed and ready to go. I should have told them last week when they were going on about Christmas and how good it was going to be with the whole family together again. This was the same conversation that we'd had every single year, and they never disappointed with their attempts to make every single year different.

Christmas was a big thing for my family in Chicago. Everyone from my cousins, to aunts, uncles, and anyone who was blood-related or married to a member of the family would show up, then we would spend a week at my parents' house, which was big. My parents had done well for themselves over the years, and their house was something that they were proud of. My dad had built it with his own hands.

"What do you mean that you're not coming here for Christmas? You won't see everyone. If Dominic wants to spend it in Alaska doing whatever he does, then so be it!" Dad announced as he took the phone from Mom. Something I was hoping that he wouldn't do.

"Amber. Really, sis? You're not coming?" my little sister, Melanie, purred as Dad handed her the phone. My family was not going to let me forget it. But they had to understand, and I'd told Melanie already that I'd been dating Dominic for three years and I wanted to take it to the next level. I wasn't an old-fashion type of girl, and I'd bought the ring and I was getting down on that one knee and proposing to him.

It was time.

Our time.

I'd planned it all, and when he said that he had to work on the rig the day after Christmas, I told him that he shouldn't worry about a thing, that my family would understand.

A lie.

Dad hated Dominic; he said that a man who couldn't settle on a career at the age of thirty would never settle down and that I was wasting my time.

He didn't know Dominic as I did. If he did, then he would understand that it was difficult for him growing up in an orphanage and that Dominic still had nightmares about his time there. He didn't speak about it, but his childhood still haunted him.

"Amber. I know you have this thing all planned out. Look, we'll speak on Christmas Day and you'll be missed, but enjoy it."

I could hear Mom and Dad question what my sister meant by "planned," but no doubt she could handle it. Unlike me, after university, Melanie moved back to Chicago, whereas I loved LA too much to think about ever leaving it. Besides, I got a job in a fantastic advertising firm and I've been climbing the ladder ever since.

I was hard-working and determined, which was why I checked my case and the details of my flight one more time. I knew that this was going to be a Christmas to remember. My parents would forgive me, and most of all, they'd see how happy I was with Dominic. That part, I was confident about.

*E*ight and a half hours later and I was finally in Fairbanks. The flights had been smooth, and knowing that everything was going according to plan gave me even more confidence to carry it out.

I smiled as the taxi driver gave me the lowdown on the town. As soon as I told him where I was heading, he seemed to know the place quite well. He even knew Dominic, which I found quite weird, because Dominic had only been here a couple of weeks.

He was chatty, and as a coincidence we were the same age. He had the same dark hair and matching eyes as Dominic, minus the pale skin.

"How exactly do you know Dominic Russell?" I said as I handed him some bills to pay the fare.

I realized I'd replayed how this was all going to work out as part of my plan; the nerves were starting to take hold of me.

I tended to pay in cash most of the time, whenever I could. Dominic said that I was old fashioned. I was about some things but not everything, which was why I was proposing to him and not waiting for him to ask me.

"D and I went to school together. Anyway, here we are. I've got another job. Tell him that I'll meet him later in the pub."

He jumped out of the taxi and then started to put my bags on the curb.

"Will D come out and help you with them, or do you want me to take them up?"

I shook my head, noticing that we weren't at the inn—the one that I told him to take me to—but at a house.

"No," I whispered.

He offered me a friendly smile, adjusting his green wooly hat, then headed back into his taxi.

Something was wrong.

Very wrong.

Dominic had said he was at the Fairbanks Inn, but as I told the driver I was going to meet Dominic, he'd brought me here. I headed to the front door, but before I got there, the door swung open.

"Hun, were you expecting someone?"

It was Dominic.

Hun?

He wasn't referring to me. Then a familiar voice answered.

"No. Why, babes?"

Shit and double shit.

The person who responded just happened to be my best friend, Gail.

"Amber. What are you—Dominic did you know?"

He didn't say a word. I looked into his eyes and realized that Dad was right, I'd been a fool.

"Dominic, darling, close the door, you'll let the cold air in. I saw Austin's taxi outside. Who are you?" the grey-haired woman said as she came to the door.

"Amber."

"Well, Dominic, let Amber in. It's freezing to be outside like this."

"Yes, Mom," were the last words I heard escape Dominic's mouth before it went dark and I realized that I'd made a big mistake.

A fucking big one.

2
BEAU

The fucking judge was on crack. *Community service.* We just got a DUI. I didn't want to spend any longer in this damn town than we needed to, and neither did my brothers. We only came here to put our uncle Fred's house on the market before Christmas. Since Mom died last year, he'd cut all communication and had been living like a recluse. He'd left everything to us, so we came here to see if there was anything we wanted to keep before it officially went on the market. But seeing as we came all the way here on our bikes, we only thought we would spend the night here. We didn't know that we had to spend the whole week. That was never in the plan.

"Stop moaning, Beau, it's not like we had any

plans," Adrian said as he headed to the kitchen, no doubt to open the fridge and complain that it was empty. He'd done that twice already whilst watching the game. My brothers both loved football, whereas I was more of a baseball fan.

"Yeah, still nothing in there since you looked twenty minutes ago."

"You're not fucking doing anything, Beau. Why not go out and get us some beers and something to eat?"

"Why don't I just…"

I imitated him with an annoying voice

"Stop it, Beau, and stop being a dick. Seriously, you're not doing anything, there's nothing wrong with just heading to the store."

There's nothing wrong with it. I never said there was, but that didn't mean I wanted to do it. I was thirty next year, but it didn't mean they could boss me around, as much as they tried to.

"Maybe after this community service is finished, we should go our separate ways."

Adrian stood up and then started massaging his beard, something he'd grown so no one mistook him for Austin. They both had blue eyes and dark hair, and they'd spent their whole lives reinventing themselves so people knew the difference between them.

I knew straight away who was who from the day they were born. Or so Mom told me. She used to tell me a lot of things. I realized at this moment that my issue wasn't so much my brothers, but they hardly spoke about Mom. She was dead, and it was as if they had forgotten about her.

I hadn't.

I never would.

"Fine, I'll go to the store so you can watch your precious football."

They nodded their heads in agreement, another thing that bugged me about them. At times I felt that as much as they wanted to be different, they were more alike than they ever knew. I didn't care as I grabbed my wallet, keys, and helmet and headed to the door.

I could hear one of them yelling, "But we need to tell him what we want!"

They would get whatever I brought back, if I came back. I felt like just hopping on my bike and getting as far away from here as possible.

As I revved up my Harley, I remembered the reason that I couldn't fucking do that.

DUI.

I had to come back, even if I didn't feel like it. Fuck!

~

I was about halfway to the store, when I saw the strangest thing ever. A woman —she must have been around five-four—kicking the shit out of her suitcase. The roads were empty, which was expected at this time of night. Most of the locals were in the bars or at home, getting ready for Christmas Eve tomorrow.

I just hoped that the store was open.

I didn't know when I turned into a fucking Good Samaritan, but I decided to park the bike and find out if she needed help.

Her red hair, looking like fire as it escaped her wooly white hat, matched her coat. As I approached her, I became nervous that I could end up with the same fate as the case.

"Slow down. I'm sure it's not that bad." I smiled as I approached her.

"Bad? It's fucking bad. Fucking, shitty bad!" she cursed as she kicked the case even harder. She was a tough lady. She didn't even look at me as she took all her frustration out on her case.

"I hate him! I fucking hate him!" she yelled at the top of her lungs, giving her case a rest.

"Whoever he is, I'm sure he's in a better state than the case."

"You would say that; you're a man. You're all the fucking same."

I shook my head, thinking as much as I loved redheads, especially with emerald eyes that sparkled the way hers did, I didn't like crazy ones.

I decided to do what I did best.

Leave.

I turned to face the bike, then I heard her panting close to me.

"Sorry. I shouldn't have… It's been a crap night."

I spun round to face the case. Thinking it was a crap night seemed to be an understatement.

"Yeah, I'll say that." I tilted my head and noted that not only was her case completely broken but the contents in it were trashed too.

"I'm sure he's not worth ruining your clothes."

"He's not worth the air that he fucking breathes."

Damn! She had fire and a potty mouth. I loved women with potty mouths, which I'd never come across, especially here in Fairbanks.

"You're not from around here."

"Neither are you! And so fucking what? What if I'm not from here? I shouldn't have come. I should have gone to Chicago. Oh no…" She kept on ranting as she spun herself around, then kept on repeating the same thing over and over again. "Chicago! Chicago! What the fuck am I going to do?"

She lost her balance and, being a knight on a fucking moto, I grabbed her so she wouldn't fall.

"Oh my," she said as our eyes locked. I helped her up and then the realization of why I stopped in the first place hit me. As my cock started to extend as I inhaled her sweet perfume. A sexy, red-haired vixen with a potty mouth.

"So, I'll leave you to it," I croaked, trying to keep a little dignity and walk away from her.

I adjusted my pants, but then she smiled as if she knew what she'd done. My face was bright red, but it was clear what was going on.

"It's good to know that someone still finds me attraction. I was thinking there's something really wrong with me. Never mind. I'll just stay here, under my clothes."

"What?"

There was no more feeling like bending her

over my bike and doing dirty things to her, I now wanted to be the good guy. You know, the one my brothers said I could never be, not in a million years.

"I found out that my boyfriend, whom I was going to propose to on Christmas night—"

I started to chuckle, and she put her hands on her hips, as if I'd done something wrong.

"What?"

"A hot-looking chick like you, needing to propose to anyone? He's a fucking fool."

"Well, that fool is with my best friend."

"Ouch."

She nodded in agreement. "Yes, ouch. And I can't get back home. The fucking airlines are booked. There are no cars. Believe me, I've fucking tried. I just want to get there so I can burn all his things. Burn them to the fucking ground!"

"Come here. Let's get your things."

I had turned into a knight overnight, because everything I was doing and saying wasn't fucking me. It wasn't me at all. I'd been called selfish more times by my brothers than I could remember, and here I was helping her out, when I should have been going to the store. I managed to get some rope off my bike and tie up the case. Luckily it wasn't big, and with my spare helmet she would stay with us for Christmas.

I wasn't just trying to be a Good Samaritan, I confessed to myself. I hoped I would be rewarded for this good deed, from the waist downward.

3
ADRIAN

Austin and I felt like crap about the way Beau left. Neither of us wanted to watch the game anymore because he'd left such a bad taste in our mouths.

"I've even lost my fucking appetite."

Austin nodded in agreement.

"We thought that Mom dying would bring us closer together." I sighed as I got up and once again checked the empty fridge.

"Yeah, but we've been separated for so long. Maybe getting the bikes and going cross country was a bad idea. Beau's been a loner; always has been, even when we were kids."

We both felt guilty that we had another brother but always acted as if we only had each other.

Austin and I connected in so many ways. Mom said it was because we took after her, whereas Beau took after his dad.

The door swung open, and both Austin and I jumped up.

Beau walked in with a smile on his face. Then I heard someone behind him and realized what he was smiling about.

"I found her on the street, kicking her case, and decided that she couldn't stay out there for Christmas."

I shook my head in agreement, surprised that he stopped and even decided to help her out.

"Of course not." Austin beamed, walking up to Beau and helping with what looked like a broken case and some clothes.

She held clothes in her arms too.

"I'm sorry, I didn't mean to invade your Christmas," she whimpered, her head covered with a white hood with little threads of ginger hair sticking out. I couldn't make out if she was a grown woman or a teen because of the way she spoke.

As she took off her hood and dumped the clothes on the table, as if this was her house, I realized the reason Beau had stopped. He had this fetish for red heads.

Crazy!

But every girl he'd introduced us to, which I could count on one hand, had all been reds.

"Amber," she said as she stretched out her hand to shake it. She was formal, and I could tell but the way she repeated the same with Austin and then took her clothes and started to organize them, she was a little bit of a neat freak too.

"Why is your case broken and your clothes all ruined?" I asked, thinking it was a little weird.

"Bro, don't worry about it. Make Amber feel at home, and she can even stay in the guest room. I'll be off to the store, be back in a few minutes."

Beau gave his instructions, assured Amber that she was in good hands, and the same guy that didn't want to go to the store had all of a sudden become a prince with good manners.

Maybe I knew my brother a lot better than I thought I did, as he waved and winked at me.

"The rest is in the hallway, but don't worry," muttered Amber. "I'll sort it all out and then I won't be in your way. You don't have to worry about me."

Austin and I exchanged a look. No longer was she talking with confidence. As she folded her clothes, I could tell she was about to cry at any moment.

"We're not that bad," I reassured her, as Austin signaled that he was going to check the room. No doubt to change the sheets and shit. We didn't think that we would be here this long. Then again, since Mom died, we stopped making plans; we just went with the flow.

"You seem nice, but your brother, Beau, seems a bit uptight."

"Well, he helped you out, so you must have affected him."

She giggled, then blushed as she started to take off her coat. I was confused for a second, then I could only think of one reason she would blush like that. Beau had a boner when he was with her or even tried something with her.

"Did my brother do something to you?"

She raised an eyebrow as if she were completely confused, so my question must have come out wrong. As she faced me, I couldn't help but think of a way to reword it, as much as I was tempted to carry out the dirty thoughts myself that my brother must have had when he met her.

"He gave me a ride. He was a perfect gentleman. Until he turned his back and was going to leave me there, but then I managed to convince him to give me a ride."

"I don't know how you managed the case and clothes on the Harley."

She nodded.

I motioned for her to follow me upstairs after Austin gave the all-clear for her to go up there. "Let me help you with all this."

I took the clothes out of her hands, then I remembered her case, but as we arrived at the room, I noticed that Austin had already taken care of it.

"Your brother doesn't say much?" Amber asked as we stood at the door.

That was when I took in all her features. Her subtle perfume seemed to entice me as she stood so near. She was wearing a black polo jersey and matching pants that hugged her figure, emphasizing her small waist, wide hips, and ample breasts.

I found myself like a schoolboy as I tried to speak. Tongue tied.

"This is my room?"

I nodded, finding myself speechless as she entered. It was as if she were taunting me as she walked around the room.

"This room is beautiful. I can see the whole town from here. Well, not the whole town, and the sea too. What a guest room."

It was breathtaking, watching her move around

the room. "What were you doing? Kicking the case and out there in the cold?"

Her smile turned to a frown. She sat on the edge of the bed, and I did the same.

"I went to surprise my ex. He wasn't my ex at the time, but he said that he had to work here and then I find him with my best friend."

"Oh."

I didn't know what more to say on the subject.

She seemed distraught as she faced me. "But that wasn't the worst part."

Could it really get any worse?

"I found out that everything he'd ever told me was a lie. His parents are very much alive. He wasn't brought up in an orphanage. They live here, and the three years we'd dated, the two years we'd lived together, he kept on lying to me. What's wrong with me? Why would someone do that?"

I shook my head, unclear why anyone would do that to her, let alone cheat on her. "Men are dogs!"

She laughed, which was the reaction that I wanted to get from her.

"Some don't know a good thing until it's gone."

She shrugged, acting as if she wasn't in agreement. I did something I was sure would convince her.

I turned her face toward me, with just a touch of my finger. She moved, and I could feel her breath racing as she did it, then I waited for a second to see if she would resist, but she didn't. No more was she crying but holding on to my palm, as if she was encouraging me to kiss her. I'd wanted those sweet lips from the moment she came into this house.

I used my tongue to lace her bottom lip, then she closed her eyes.

I shouldn't be taking advantage of her in her delicate state, but I couldn't help it.

I wanted her so badly, and the boner that I thought Beau had when he'd met her was taking over my mind. I was giving her butterfly kisses, rather than going for a dramatic lip-lock action so that we could get down and dirty. I didn't want that from her; I wanted her to feel better. I could feel it working, as she made light moans as I barely brushed my lips against hers. It was as if she were hypnotized as she titled her head to the side as if she'd lost complete control.

4
AMBER

One minute he was helping me up the stairs with my clothes, and the next he had his hands on me. His hand pressed gently into my lower back, then roughly slid down, his intention clear, as his hand moved toward my butt. I should have asked where his brother was, but the fact that he wanted me was enough for me to crave more, as the heat from his hand burned through my pants and into my skin. Every muscle in my body tensed as I thought about my ex and how he had me pleading for more in the bedroom.

This biker was the complete opposite. He made me feel like a woman, not some idiot who chased after someone who lied to them from the get-go.

My nipples hardened as I clenched my jaw

while my heart pounded in my chest. Neither of us said a word as his hand moved down to my thigh while caressing it.

"Face the other way," he commanded, and I did as he said.

As I spun around, his hand skimmed across me and slid down to my hip. His fingertips spread on my lower back, all the way, as he took my pants off and slowly shifted my feet to take off my socks, leaving me half naked.

A muscle twitched in his jaw as his thumb began to move, sliding back and forth.

I didn't say a word as my insides twisted with the sensation of his rough fingers. They weren't smooth, but the fingers of a man who worked, as if he did construction or something.

His fingers started to pinch my skin. I opened my eyes for a split second and it was then that I noticed he was watching me.

I sucked in a sharp breath, feeling as if I was melting from the outside to the inside.

There was a heavy ache between my legs, because he wasn't touching me where I wanted him to. No, he kept his hands going up and down the inside of my thighs, as if he were getting off just watching me.

Then he slowly moved a finger to the entrance of my dripping pussy.

"You're so fucking wet, and we haven't even started yet!"

Before I could even respond, his brother walked in—his twin.

He licked his lip as he came closer. "Shit, you were starting the party without me?"

I shook my head, thinking that I was at the mercy of not one biker but two.

"Do you mind if I join in, darling?"

He winked, and I found myself with not only one set of hands on my body but two.

I glanced down at Adrian's lap and I could see his dick straining against his pants. Then he pulled my hips roughly against him, lifting me up, but he didn't put me on the bed. I heard Austin shove the contents of the side table in the room, which smashed against the floor. My legs spread open and I groaned as I was placed on the table, and Austin was on the other side, tugging at my polo neck.

"Have you ever fucked a biker before?" Austin growled as he tossed my jersey to the side. Everything was happening so fast, I felt if they did it slowly, then I would come to my boring senses and stop them.

My head fell to the side as I leaned back on my elbows.

"Shit, look what the jersey was hiding!" Austin motioned to Adrian.

"You've got one hot body, sexy lady!"

Sexy?

No one had ever called me that before.

Sensible, attractive, wife-worthy. But sexy? No, that wasn't me, that was my best friend, Gail. Maybe that was why my ex had hooked up with her. Then again, he was now my ex, and she was my ex-best friend. I was about to be ridden by two hotties, and instead of enjoying it all, I was too busy thinking about my painful past.

Austin slid his hands up my ribs and then over my breasts.

"Adrian, you take care of the bottom half, and I'll satisfy her from the waist upward."

Oh my!

Austin's thumbs slipped back and forth across my taut nipples and his dark stare was fixated on my expression. I could only keep my eyes open for a split second, as suddenly he wasn't rubbing it over my bra. One hand was at the back of my clasp as he unattached my bra and started to work his way over my aching nipples, my bra a thing of the past.

I felt like a bad girl, as they'd described themselves as dirty bikers, knowing that there was a bed next to the table—but they didn't want me on the bed. No, they wanted me one the table.

Austin's hands were big and rough, but not painful, as he backed off, then pushed his palms deeper, wanting more and harder.

He leaned closer and bit my shoulder.

Shit, I'd never been bitten before.

"You want it rough, don't you?"

"Yes, please. You don't need a condom," I whimpered, not recognizing the sound of my own voice. I wanted to explain about being on the pill, but then I found myself hardly being able to speak.

I could see Adrian's length in front of me, and as I was about to take off the belt of his pants, Adrian started to work me as Austin had said he should, because before he had one hand just racing up and down the inside of my thigh. But as Adrian growled, I realized that he was taking off his pants so that he could work the other side of me. The inside.

"Arrh!" I cried out, as he shoved his cock inside of me.

Adrian's hips slapped against my thighs, driving deeper inside me.

"You've never been fucked like this, have you?"

I shook my head, unable to answer, as Austin was bent over and sucking on my tits, teasing them with nibbling bites. Every part of my body was on fire.

Then, as Adrian continued to jerk and drive deeper into me, he would move my ankle to one side, as if he was trying to get his cock to fill every part of my wet pussy. Sometimes he would hold me still against his hips, then he would move side to side.

Austin controlled my body, as he had said from the top upward, by using one hand to hold on to my wrists. I had no control as he used his other to grip on to one breast, bite then suck the nipple, then he would move his finger around the whole globe of my breast.

I screamed so loud that it frightened me, and I was worried that they would stop, but their moans and groans told me they enjoyed it even more.

"This is why we share women. We love making them come in more ways than they ever imagined," Adrian said on a groan.

Then it hit me.

They were experts in this; they'd done it so many times.

The only thing I could move was my head as I closed my eyes. With the rhythm of Adrian fucking me so raw, I couldn't help but come so close so quickly, even though I didn't want it to end.

"Now, now, little lady. No one said you could come…" Adrian snarled as his cock was no longer filling me up but leaving a vacant space in between my legs.

"Don't stop! I was so close."

He started to chuckle. "Beg. Beg me to make you fucking come. You dirty girl!"

"Make me come. Just don't stop."

No more was Austin sucking my breasts. No more were hands on my body. They'd both moved away.

Bastards!

"You're fucking bastards!"

It was as if Austin's eyes went dark, as he moved and switched places with his brother. His fucking cock was so fucking big, long and thick.

It was so enormous that I opened my mouth wide at the shock of it.

He reached around, moving his fingertips across my clit, and then found the right rhythm, the same as Adrian who was now massaging my breasts and fucking his tongue in my mouth.

I started to come once again. It was as if I hadn't stopped, as I felt my legs being lifted and put on top of Austin's shoulders. Then he squeezed his cock into my pussy, and I gasped as he pushed my legs together.

Unlike his brother, Austin's rhythm was a lot slower. They were moving at the same pace as he filled my walls, and I couldn't hold back any longer as I started to cry.

I clutched onto Adrian's hands so tightly as my body quaked as I reached my climax, and the whole rush took over me. Adrian broke away from our kiss, allowing me to gasp for air. I felt as if it wasn't enough and I needed more, as if all the oxygen had been taken out of the atmosphere. When it subsided, I felt arms underneath my body. I turned my head to see that it was Adrian smiling, his blue eyes glowing as he shifted me from the table to the bed.

"You get some rest, little lady. Because we'll be doing that all over again."

"I need some water."

"On it," Austin called from behind us.

I smiled as I felt the covers being tugged from the side, then something slid between my legs. I thought it must be a towel, but I was too tired to open my eyes.

I wanted water at first, but Adrian said that I would get some rest. I smiled as the covers were pulled over me, not at the idea of getting some rest, but the thought of doing it all over again, not just with one biker but with two.

5
BEAU

"Anyone at home?" I shouted out as I helped the taxi driver with the bags. "Austin? Adrian? Give us a hand."

There was no response, so I called out once again. This time, they both responded in unison.

"Coming!"

As I headed back inside, they both came running down the stairs, faces flushed, topless, with big fucking grins on their faces.

Grins that made me grab Austin by the arm roughly. "Where's Amber?"

"In bed!"

Then he wriggled his arm away from me. I rushed up the stairs, thinking they could pay for the fucking taxi, then swung the door open.

Sure enough, she was in bed. But, not only in bed; she was naked too. It was as if not only Adrian got a taste of her but Austin too.

I fucking hated them. I ran back down the stairs and I could see that they had finished with the taxi outside. "What the fuck? So I bring her home and what, you both fuck her?"

"Shh, calm down, Beau!" Adrian said as he yanked his arm away from me.

"Don't tell me to fucking calm down. You're out of order!"

My anger took over my body as I gripped my fist, then smashed into my brother's face.

"What the fuck!" Adrian shouted from the other side of the kitchen. He needed a piece of this too. They both did, because they were out of order.

I clenched my fist once again, but Adrian was too quick. He didn't give me a chance to smash his face before he did the same to me.

"Beau, you need to fucking calm down!"

"Right on my fucking nose!" Austin yelled as he held his nose, blood starting to spurt out.

"You're acting as if she's your fucking property and we illegally trespassed on it."

"I'm no one's fucking property and no one did anything that I didn't want to happen. I'm out of here. I thought you guys were nice, but you're all the same! All the fucking same!" Amber yelled.

She ran down the stairs butt naked, as though she had heard our screams and came out of her bed. Now she was going back up the stairs.

"I'll speak to her," Adrian offered, obviously thinking that if anyone could convince her to stay, it was him.

I was the one who found her, and I would fix it. Even if it was a matter of life or death.

6
AMBER

I could hear footsteps coming up the stairs, just in time for me to find my underwear, but nothing more. I must admit that I was in desperate need of a shower before I got busy with the brothers, and even more so now.

"You can't convince me," I shouted, not caring who was by the door. "I'm leaving!"

"Slow down, tiger. I can understand you being scared, but if you just hear me out, then I can explain a few things."

I spun around to remind myself why I ended up in bed with not only one brother but two. Adrian's muscular frame made me once again want to run my hands all over it.

He was so sexy.

"We've been separated for the past five years. Our mom died, and this is what brought us together."

I nodded, thinking that I couldn't deal with all this family drama when I had my mess to sort out. I was cold, and my nipples were erect, but I didn't know if it was from the hot, sexy biker in front of me or the cold.

"You see, Austin and I have the same dad, but Beau's is different. Ours died from cancer around five years ago. Beau didn't even bother turning up at the funeral."

"Shit, that's rough."

He shrugged. "No, our dad was an ass to him. Sent him away to our grandma's and did everything he could possibly do to keep him out of his sight. He hated him, because he was obsessed with the idea that Mom was still in love with his dad and Beau was a spitting image of him."

"That's no excuse, he was a kid."

Adrian shook his head. "I wasn't excusing, just explaining it. Anyway, our uncle died, and we just came here to put the house on the market and see the place for the last time. It's the first time in five years we've been together and we went a bit crazy. Beau had a shitload of parking tickets to pay, then I got a DUI and the judge said we had a shitload of community service hours to do this Christmas. So, that's our plan for tomorrow, being Santa's helpers and going round to local hospitals."

I started to laugh. "You're kidding me. On your bikes?"

"Yeah, like fucking Santa's dirty bikers."

I nodded as I realized that it had a ring to it.

"Is it safe to come in?" Beau asked.

"Have you calmed down?" I replied, thinking that if he wasn't down with me staying, then I wasn't going to do it. I didn't want to cause problems between brothers, and by the sound of things, they'd only just made amends. "Only if you don't hit anyone or attack one of your brothers."

I swung on my jersey, thinking that I didn't need a bra right now. It felt like the least of my worries.

"No, Scout's honor," Beau said as he put his hand on his heart.

"You were never in the Scouts, and if you were, then you would have been kicked out."

"More like thrown out!" Austin corrected Adrian while both their attentions turned to Beau.

Oh, that was harsh, but these guys were funny, and right now I could do with some laughter.

Spending Christmas with them wouldn't be as

hard, or bad, as I'd thought it would be a few minutes ago. The fighting would probably help them get it off their chest, and I could cool down the temperature when things got heated. This was going to be a Christmas to remember, in all the dirty ways.

~

I was tired. No, I was exhausted, and the guys had said they would need to do rounds at different hospitals and deliver Christmas gifts. I didn't even know it was a thing.

Adrian had told me the craziest thing, and I couldn't stop laughing. I went down the stairs to find the brothers and ask them if it was true.

"So, let me get this straight. You and Adrian are part of the Devil's Rejects Motorcycle Club?" I was dressed in white today, from a white jersey to matching jeans.

"Yes, Adrian and I are called Rider and Rock."

I felt as if I was going to have a heart attack; hearing his confession just made me laugh even more.

"I know, pathetic, right?" Beau asked as he put down his mug of coffee, as he decided to join in the conversation. I'd been watching him ever since he had his little blowout. He'd calmed down somewhat, which didn't make me feel so bad about staying.

"But a little bird tells me that you were part of an MC too."

Before Beau could even answer, Adrian opened his mouth to speak. "And he was called Gears in the Eagle MC."

"Gears!" I shook my head, thinking he would deny it, but his dark eyes cut to mine and I couldn't help but laugh some more. "So, wait. I'm with Rock, Rider, and Gears. Where's fucking Brakes?"

We all laughed in unison at the idea of it. I knew that I was mocking them, and this was probably some underground dark world to them, but to me it was a whole new world. One that they were exposing me to over Christmas.

"Well, you can laugh, but look what I managed to get for you this morning," Austin said as he waved an elf outfit in front of me.

I stopped laughing. For some reason, they said I could go with them, and I did like the idea of it. They were right; I had to go, and it made sense for me to do it as an elf.

"I'm not a costume type of girl," I confessed, thinking they wouldn't exactly find me interesting if they knew that back home I was as boring as they came.

"When you're riding on one of these…" Adrian smiled, as he dragged me by my hand to the driveway.

"A fucking sleigh? You've got to be kidding me!" There was a sleigh with a couple of horses and loads of presents in sacks. I lifted the sacks and saw the presents were in there. These guys were taking their job seriously. I smiled as I felt like a kid, one who would see this riding to the hospital of doom where I'd spend my Christmas and then seeing this and then an elf and not just one Santa but three.

"How did you pull this off?"

"When you've got money, then anything's possible," Beau replied.

Yeah, I'd heard it a million times, even in my job. He wasn't being arrogant but pointing out the obvious.

"When are we leaving?"

"You've got twenty minutes to get ready, and we have to put on our wigs and beards. Well, not all of us. Beau's beard is longer than our wigs!" Adrian chuckled as he moved back inside the house.

Twenty minutes, I thought as I jumped up and down and then hurried into the house to get ready.

Yesterday, I thought this would be the worst Christmas of my life, but the idea of giving would make it special. I loved the idea of the kids being happy on this day. This was what Christmas was about—the kids.

7
AUSTIN

"Seeing the smiles on those kids' faces was completely priceless. Especially Zak's."

Our eyes met with sadness as he mentioned Zak.

He was a six-year-old who had cancer practically his whole life. He'd been in and out of the hospital so many times that the nurse told us that most likely this would be his last Christmas. Leukemia had taken over his whole body and nothing had worked from the bone marrow transplant to chemo. The little boy had no hair and was as white as snow, but from the moment he received his gift, his dark eyes lit up.

"I've never done any charity work," Amber said with tears in her eyes. No doubt, she was still feeling emotional about Zak.

I turned to face Amber, surprised at her confession. "I had you down as Ms. Goody Two-shoes. Helping the homeless and all that."

She sighed. "I used to do all that. Then Dominic, my ex, told me that the homeless were lazy people. People who didn't want to work. That I shouldn't be helping out at the shelter. I did everything he asked me to do."

"He sounds like a piece of work," Beau said as he crossed his arms.

I knew he was getting annoyed.

"A lot of the guys that were part of our MC were once homeless," Beau continued. "The MC gave them life and purpose when they were completely lost. Why did you listen to the jerk?"

She took in a deep breath, avoiding my eyes, but all eyes were on her. Adrian was seated on the other side of the sofa, and we weren't facing the TV, even though we decided to watch a Christmas movie before hitting the sack.

"It's like, I had the perfect job. The perfect life. And all I needed was the perfect boyfriend. Dominic ticked all the boxes."

"You had a list?" Beau asked, surprised, his eyes nearly ready to pop out of his head.

I wasn't surprised that she had a list. I knew she

was the organized type from the moment she entered this house.

"Did you have a to-do list for fucking too?" Beau chuckled, but Amber wasn't laughing as she bit her lip and then abruptly stood up.

"Why do you always have to be a jerk?" I asked Beau as I grabbed her arm and motioned for her to sit down.

"I'll get the drinks and popcorn." Adrian smiled at Amber before heading to the kitchen.

She relaxed a bit, but I could tell she was annoyed by Beau's comment.

"Find something." I handed her the remote and headed to the kitchen to join my brothers.

"Why do you have to be such a jerk?" I asked Beau, and Adrian repeated the question, confirming what I'd already suspected—that he was just as annoyed as I was.

"You guys run around her as if she's Ms. Goody-two shoes," muttered Beau.

I shook my head. "No. No one's fucking perfect. Not her. Not us. Not anyone. She's had a rough time. She's not with her family, her ex, or her best friend."

"Realistically, she's better off without them," Beau said as he took the beers from the fridge.

At last, we can have something stronger than coffee and sodas. It'd been a long day, but Amber was right. Seeing those kids' faces had been worth the community service. I decided, like Adrian, that next year we would do the same thing.

We'll ask Beau if he wants to join us.

I hope he does.

I hope after all is said and done we can still be a family.

One can fucking hope.

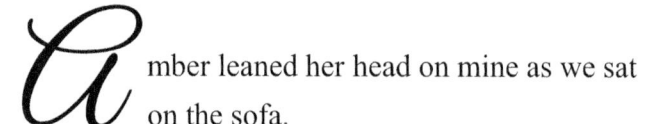

~

Amber leaned her head on mine as we sat on the sofa.

Beau whispered from the other side of me, "When she wakes up, tell her tomorrow night, she's mine. You and Adrian have had fun. Tomorrow's my turn." Then he got off the sofa and left my side. I didn't ask where he was going or argue with him, because in a way he was right. It wasn't fair to act as if Amber was in this house for the pair of us. Adrian and I did everything together, but maybe Amber could be the person we needed in our lives to break that rule.

Before she came here, we were looking at going

our separate ways. The idea we had to be with our brother seemed to be over before it had even begun. Now, maybe there was a chance for us to stay together, and she was the reason.

Adrian and I had shared one woman before, and it was the best decision that we'd ever made until things got out of control. We got jealous about the wrong things, and she'd left. This time will be different, because we would agree on the rules.

Maybe Beau should have his turn and it would work out for the best.

Amber would decide which way she wanted to roll.

8
BEAU

As soon as she shut the door to her room, I moved behind the door. She couldn't know I was there.

"I know you're there."

The room was dark, but it sounded as if she was smirking as she said it. Not one but both of my brothers had tasted her. It wasn't fair, and I'd patiently waited for Christmas to be over before coming in here for my turn.

I grabbed her and pinned her against the door. She pulled away.

"Don't move!" I demanded, then she stopped trying to be set free. "We both know that it's my turn."

"I'm not some fucking toy that you can each have a turn to play with on Christmas."

"So you're a tease, then?"

Our lips were so close that I could kiss her. I wanted her to tell me no, to tell me to move away.

I exhaled, bending to her neck. "Tell me to go away. Tell me that you don't want this."

Her breathing was now coming in sharp bursts, and I could feel the heat from her body warming mine, telling me something completely different.

I licked her jaw before covering her lips with mine. My cock hardened at the idea of kissing those sweet oval lips. I started to imagine them wrapped around my cock, and it made me hard in an instant.

"You want this just as much as I do. The older brother. The one with the bigger cock. What he's like?"

"You flatter yourself. Austin has a big cock too."

"Not like mine!"

She gasped and her lips wrapped around mine, as if she was telling me with her body language that she wanted this, and there was no holding back.

Her hands found their way to my hair as she pressed in closer to my arousal. I put my hands on her shoulders, then looked into her eyes. The dim moonlight reflected into the room and I could see there was a look of excitement written all over her face.

I pulled back so that I could undress her. As she lifted her dress, I helped her by yanking it off her. Then I tossed it to the side.

She was in her underwear, so I tugged at the back of her and unclasped her bra.

"Beautiful," I moaned as she was half-naked.

Then I yanked off her thong, like a fucking caveman.

I lifted my hand to her head, then moved her around so that she was pressed up against the door. I gave her wet, hot kisses down her spine as my lips pressed into her delicate skin. I grabbed her ass tightly and pressed into her flesh.

"Fuck!" she shouted.

I wanted her to know that, unlike my brothers, I was far from a fucking gentleman. "You enjoyed that didn't you?"

She said nothing, so I did it again.

"No…" She quivered, letting me know that she was lying.

I smacked her butt hard, and this time I bit her, and she moaned with pleasure. I slid my hand around her waist and stomach, wanting to feel every piece of her body not only with my hands, but with my mouth too.

She was still standing upright. I slipped my finger down until it rested on her clit.

The pressure of my touch caused her to grab a hold of my hand and guide me to it, slowly moving it up and down.

"You're loving it, aren't you?"

I didn't need verbal confirmation, because her body was telling me everything I needed to know. I changed the pressure of my fingers, pressing and then releasing them. I knew she wanted fucking more.

I pushed my finger inside of her more, and she pressed her back into me.

All I could hear were soft moans as I released her, as if she wanted more but was too shy to say it.

I hadn't taken a thing off. I had no intention of doing so until she begged me to take her. I plunged my fingers in and out of her and then decided to pinch her nipple. That was when she moaned loudly and I could feel her legs going weak.

I could have told her that she didn't have to worry. I had told my brothers it was my turn and that I wanted her alone.

They didn't argue or even put up a fight. If

anything, Austin told me to enjoy her. He thought that she would resist, that she wouldn't want me, but he was fucking wrong.

She was behaving far from it.

I rolled my thumb over her clit.

"Fuck me!" Amber cried as her legs gave way, and I found myself having to stop her from falling.

I moved her to the bed, carrying her as if she were a delicate flower. I spread her legs wide apart as I stood at the foot of the bed. "Beg!"

She cried, "Arrh, I want you inside me so badly."

"Say it as if you mean it," I growled.

"I want your big, fat cock inside of me, please."

That was it. That was more to my liking. But I didn't strip off in a hurry.

I watched her wiggle on the bed, as if she couldn't hold back any longer. "Touch yourself. Like you do when you're alone."

She shook her head. "I don't. I never have."

I chuckled, until the light caught her eye and I realized that she wasn't joking. She'd never touched herself, which could only mean one thing. No man had given her such sexual desire that if they weren't around she would want to come alone. I knew one thing for sure: after her time with us, that would be a thing of the past.

Now I was naked and ready for the taking.

"Good, you're still wet," I growled as I teased my cock at her entrance. I didn't put it in but played with it. Her hands started to move toward me, as if she wanted to teach me my job.

With my other hand, I moved toward hers and held on to them tightly to stop her.

Her legs were free, so I put them under my control too, and guided her to wrap them around me.

Then, slowly, I started taking her deeper. I was aching, dying to just plunge into her, but I wanted her to have the orgasm of a lifetime. As I began to get deeper, she moaned louder every time, so close to my mouth. I loved feeling her breath against mine. As promised, my big, fat cock entered her and I could tell that it was a bit of a squeeze as she cried out.

"You okay?"

"Don't stop!"

Good, I wasn't hurting her. If anything, she was really enjoying the ride as we made music with our bodies. Then she started to jerk, but I wasn't done yet, not by a long shot. I didn't wait all this time for it to be over in a flash.

She wanted me to set her free.

Amber could fucking forget it.

This would be her first climax, then she would need another set of fingers and toes to count how many she would have before New Year's.

"Shit, I'm coming!"

"I know you are, darling. Ride through it. Ride with me."

And like that, that was exactly what she did. No longer was she trying to be in control or fight it; she was riding through her climax as I'd told her to do. I enjoyed every thrust as I took complete control over her, until I couldn't hold back any longer.

I hated my body for letting me down and for surrendering to my climax. As my body started to jerk uncontrollably and I thrust quicker and deeper, no more in control, my cum shot out of me and into her sweet pussy.

I collapsed onto her body as I let go of her hands. We were both panting and trying to recover, until I shifted my weight to the other side of the bed.

"Fuck! That was amazing!" I yelled as I tried to get up, but every time, I sank back into the bed.

"Where are you going?" Amber asked as she moved closer.

"To my room."

"No. Don't do that. We should cuddle."

Cuddle?

Did she know who she was talking to?

She'd gone to the bathroom to get a towel, then came back and wiped us both down. Then, as she headed into the bed, she covered us with the covers and we did something that I hadn't done since I was a child. We cuddled.

9
AMBER

I sent Mom a message saying that I was safe and all was well, but I didn't tell her exactly what happened over Christmas. Part of me couldn't get it out of my mind.

My ex-boyfriend and best friend, and the fact I'd slept with not only one biker but three. Three brothers who seemed to be somewhat estranged, something that didn't exist in my family.

"How was the call to your family?"

I sighed, thinking that all Mom and Dad could do was cheer as I told them that it was over with Dominic. Neither of them had liked him, and Dad constantly told me that I could do a lot better than him. I was stubborn and thinking about my list. The one that didn't get me anywhere but to Alaska and staying with three dirty Santas.

I sat lost in my thoughts at the breakfast table, wondering what I was going to do with my life.

"How would you feel about spending New Year's with us?" Beau frowned as the three of them joined me at the breakfast table.

"Is that what you all want?" My eyes darted across the table, and they were met with nods by not one brother but all three of them.

"Going to the hospital made us realize that life is too short. Especially seeing little Zak."

The problems with my ex.

Not spending it with my family.

They felt so irrelevant as I asked him for a hug, and he told me that he couldn't think of anything better than having a hug from a pretty elf like me.

I shed a tear. Something I never did in public. I never showed emotions, and since I'd been here, I'd kicked my case on the street, shouted at strangers, and slept with three brothers. All things that I would never usually do.

Nothing about my normal routine was a consideration.

I had a secret. One that I hadn't told them since I saw the email this morning.

"I've been sacked. I lost my job."

Their mouths dropped open. I'd made it clear that without my job, I was nothing. Yet, when I saw the email, I didn't care.

"How?"

"Why?"

I shook my head. "It doesn't matter. Life's too short. Besides, as you said, I'm thinking about Zak and I want to stay for New Year's."

"Maybe a little longer, because we have no plans."

No plans!

I used to plan when and where I would fuck, and now I was going to stay with three guys with no plans.

"It sounds like the perfect New Year to me."

"We have just one request," Beau said as he raised an eyebrow.

I could tell that he had something dirty in mind as he adjusted himself in his chair.

"You need to put the elf outfit back on. You look too hot in that."

I got up and bowed, thinking I would put on the outfit and nothing else underneath. This time I was the one winking as I turned to face them and headed up the stairs. I was going to be sore by New Year's.

And I didn't fucking care.

EPILOGUE

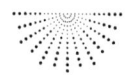

Amber

One year had passed, and I thought about the way my life had changed. It had felt like the end of the world this time last year. I'd found out my best friend and boyfriend were together, and not only that but that our whole time together had been one big lie.

I didn't know who I hated more.

Him?

Her?

Or me?

I blamed myself for introducing them and letting them fall in love. The guys made me realize that there was so much more to me. I felt as if I had run around trying to please everyone all the time.

"Are you going to sit there all day, or are you coming to eat with the rest of us?" Mom asked, smiling at me, as my parents welcomed Beau, Adrian, and Austin into the house with loving arms.

"You should have gotten yourself a real man a long time ago." My aunt Casey winked at me as she helped me put baby Dawn to rest.

She was a tough one to breastfeed. Mom said that she was a hungry baby just like me.

"Or men, in the case of Amber!"

They both chuckled as I put a blanket over Dawn and then asked my aunt the question I'd been dying all day to ask. "Auntie, why do you keep asking the boys all these questions? 'How does it work between us?' 'Don't they get jealous?' and stuff like that?"

Adrian had told me that whenever there was a quiet moment, she was cornering them to the side and interrogating them. Aunt Casey was the youngest one from my mom's side of the family. The unexpected baby, so Grandma likes to call her.

"I thought I was too old to have any more kids, then Casey popped out!"

She told the boys the story as soon as she met them, which was why she was only five years older than me at thirty.

"Because I'd heard about this sort of thing before. What do they call it? Polygram?"

"Polyamory," I corrected her.

"Anyway, I've never been a one man-one woman type of girl, and seeing you so happy, something that I never imagined happening in a million years… Well, it has got me thinking. Maybe I should go out there and get myself a polydamn!"

I shook my head at the idea of celebrating next Christmas not only with my three guys but having my aunt bringing another three guys too. Well, I decided that next year would be even more interesting than this year.

"Babes, don't worry, I've got the baby talker, which is on her stroller. We can hear her if she wakes up." Austin smiled as he took my arm and guided me to the table. Since I had Dawn and Derek, I had been an overprotective mom of twins.

"Oh, before we start, I've got some really interesting news."

My cousin Pam smirked as I sat down. "Did you know Dominic and Gail have split up? She caught him cheating."

I nodded, thinking that it should have made me happy knowing that my ex and my ex-best friend had broken up. But I smiled at my men as Mom told Aunt Casey to stop interrogating them so we could all eat. I looked at the turkey, vegetables, my whole family. The ones I regretted not spending Christmas with last year. I was happy living with my dirty bikers in Alaska and being a mother to twins. It was as if losing my job and my ex had been the best thing that had ever happened to me.

I had savings after selling my apartment in LA that I had shared with Dominic. I would figure out what to do with it, maybe when the twins were older. Right now, I was planning on having a fantastic Christmas with my immediate family, my lovers, and my kids.

ABOUT THE F*** UNDER THE MISTLETOE SERIES

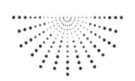

F* Under the Mistletoe is a 6 book collection series by Poppy Flynn, Sarwah Creed, Sylvie Haas, Kylie Love & Alys Fraser.**

A collection of standalone novels from New Adult, Stepbrother, OMYW, Mafia and Second Chance Romance. There is something for every reader in this amazing reverse harem series!

One-Night Stand by Sarwah Creed
I went to Vegas and hit the roulette table. I lost a bet, not to one guy but all three.

Sparkles and Spankings by Sylvie Haas

Going for top dollar at the charity auction feels like a win, but the three highest bidders have an even better proposition for me.

Basic Instinct by Poppy Flynn

A staff Christmas party in a kink dungeon is one thing... getting caught under the mistletoe by three of her colleagues? Well that was an entirely different matter!

Three Santas & I

One curvy girl, three hung Santas... Christmas will be torrid this year!

Holly's Mistletoe Mafia

When she finds herself in the wrong place at the wrong time, three Mr. Rights make Holly an offer she can't refuse.

Santa's Dirty Bikers by Sarwah Creed
Tired of being good, Amber decides to get down and dirty with Santa's bikers.

ABOUT SARWAH CREED

Sarwah Creed is the author of The FlirtChat series. When she's not writing, she's running, reading, or listening to music. She lives with her three children in Madrid.

Learn more about Sarwah by connecting with her on social media:

Newsletter ---- http://eepurl.com/g0cLoH

ABOUT THE F*** UNDER THE MISTLETOE SERIES

F* Under the Mistletoe is a 6 book collection series by Poppy Flynn, Sarwah Creed, Sylvie Haas, Kylie Love & Alys Fraser.**

A collection of standalone novels from New Adult, Stepbrother, OMYW, Mafia and Second Chance Romance. There is something for every reader in this amazing reverse harem series!

One-Night Stand by Sarwah Creed
I went to Vegas and hit the roulette table. I lost a bet, not to one guy, but all three.

Sparkles and Spankings by Sylvie Haas
Going for top dollar at the charity auction feels

like a win, but the three highest bidders have an even better proposition for me.

Basic Instinct by Poppy Flynn

A staff Christmas party in a kink dungeon is one thing... getting caught under the mistletoe by three of her colleagues? Well that was an entirely different matter!

Three Santas & I

One curvy girl, three hung Santas... Christmas will be torrid this year!

Holly's Mistletoe Mafia

When she finds herself in the wrong place at the wrong time, three Mr. Rights make Holly an offer she can't refuse.

Santa's Dirty Bikers by Sarwah Creed

Tired of being good, Amber decides to get down and dirty with Santa's bikers.

Printed in Great Britain
by Amazon